Clifford THE BIG RED DOG

CLIFFORD FOR PRESIDENT

by Acton Figueroa
Illustrated by Tom Lapadula
Based on the Scholastic book series
"Clifford The Big Red Dog"
by Norman Bridwell

0-439-69391-8

Copyright © 2004 Scholastic Ente
All rights reserved. Based on the CLIFFORD THE BIG RED DOG book serie
SCHOLASTIC and associated logos are trad
trademarks of Scholastic Inc. CLIFFORD, CLIFFORD THE E
trademarks and/or registered trademarks

10 9 8 7 6 5

Printed in the U.S.A.
First printing, October 2004

D1018656

SCHOLASTIC INC.

New York   Toronto   London   Auckland   Sydney
Mexico City   New Delhi   Hong Kong   Buenos Aires

On Monday morning, Miss Carrington's class learned about the presidential election.

"Every citizen eighteen and older can vote,"

said Miss Carrington.

"It's an important part of being a good citizen."

"People who run for president

are called *candidates*,"

said Miss Carrington.

"They promise to solve problems.

People vote for the candidate

who they think will do the best job."

I wish I was old enough to vote,

thought Emily Elizabeth.

The next day, Emily Elizabeth and Clifford

went for a walk in the park.

Every trash can was overflowing.

"That doesn't look very nice,"

said Emily Elizabeth.

The park was very messy.

There were piles of leaves

and litter everywhere.

Dead flowers drooped in their beds.

Clifford dropped a soda can in the trash.

Emily Elizabeth said, "Clifford,

if you were president of the park,

it would be clean as a whistle."

Then she had an idea!

At home, Emily Elizabeth

got out paint and paper.

"We'll have an election, Clifford," she said.

"We need a president of the park!"

Jetta saw the posters

hanging in the park.

"You'd be a great president, Mac," said Jetta.

"You're the dog for the job!"

A crowd of kids and dogs

showed up for the meeting.

"First we need to nominate two candidates," explained Emily Elizabeth.

"Then we'll have the election on Friday."

Jetta called out,

"I nominate Mac!"

Mac wagged his tail.

"I nominate Clifford!"

said Emily Elizabeth.

Then she wished Mac good luck.

"Thanks!" said Jetta.

Emily Elizabeth and Jetta

worked on posters together.

Emily Elizabeth's poster read:

CLIFFORD FOR PRESIDENT.

HE WILL CLEAN UP THE PARK!!

Jetta's poster read: VOTE FOR MAC.

HE'S THE BEST DOG!!

Jetta said, "Mac really is the best.

I'm sure he'll win."

"Clifford is a great dog, too,"

said Emily Elizabeth.

Jetta said, "Mac will be president."

"May the best dog win,"

replied Emily Elizabeth.

That night, Jetta made
a few more posters.
"Now everyone will know
you are the best, Mac!"
She hung the posters in the park.

After school on Friday,

Emily Elizabeth and Clifford

went to the park.

It was Election Day.

A crowd stood around Jetta.
"Clifford would not be
a good president!" she said.
"Mac is the best!"

Emily Elizabeth didn't say anything.

It's not nice to say bad things

about your opponent, she thought.

"Look at Clifford!" shouted Charley.

"He's cleaning the park!"

"It's time to vote!" said Charley.

He passed out slips of paper.

"Check off the name of the dog

who will be the best president."

After everyone had voted,

Charley counted the ballots.

Everybody waited for the results.

Clifford won!

He gave Mac a friendly slurp.

"Clifford will be a good president,"

said Emily Elizabeth.

"Mac can be vice president!"

Hooray for President Clifford!

Do You Remember?

Circle the right answer.

1. Who decided to have an election for president of the park?
   a. Jetta
   b. Emily Elizabeth
   c. Charley

2. What did Clifford do after he won?
   a. He cleaned up the park.
   b. He slurped Emily Elizabeth.
   c. He slurped Mac.

Which happened first?

Which happened next?

Which happened last?

Write a 1, 2, or 3 in the space after each sentence.

Jetta made posters. _____

Clifford put a can in the trash. _____

Emily Elizabeth learned about the presidential election

in school. _____

Answers:

Emily Elizabeth learned about
the presidential election in school. (1)

Clifford put a can in the trash. (2)

Jetta made posters. (3)

1. b
2. c